THE BARISTA AND I

THE BARISTA AND I

STORIES

ANDREW SZYMANSKI

SEROTONIN | WAYSIDE

INSOMNIAC PRESS

Edited by Jon Paul Fiorentino

Library and Archives Canada Cataloguing in Publication
Szymanski, Andrew
    The barista and I / Andrew Szymanski.

Short stories.
ISBN 978-1-55483-084-8

    I. Title.

PS8637.Z96B37 2012   C813'.6   C2012-905393-7

The publisher gratefully acknowledges the support of the Canada Council, the Ontario Arts Council and the Department of Canadian Heritage through the Canada Book Fund.

Printed and bound in Canada

Insomniac Press, 520 Princess Ave.
London, Ontario, Canada, N6B 2B8
www.insomniacpress.com

Contents

H<small>YDE</small> P<small>ARK</small>

I was sitting in the dark at Hyde Park because I sucked at travelling. My intention was to arrive during the late afternoon daylight hours, lounge around in the waning sunlight. Instead, after a few aimless bus rides and some meandering, I came to a bench at about 9:30 p.m. I was contemplating how being poor sucked as bats flew in aimless horizontal ovals above my head over the edge of the water.

The water looked like a huge precipice going ever deep, some curious effect from the way the lamplight played on the water. It sucked to have no one, but I was not quite lonely. I had plenty of people to correspond with. Bats played in the darkness, just out of the lamplight's reach, over the edge of the water. I hunched my shoulders in case a bat got an idea to try and fly into the side of my head.

Hyde Park was not so charming at night. The day's leisure left a kind of tangible void. I pulled a can of Coke and a Cheestrings from my backpack. It sucked to be poor, and it was worse to be lonely. I wished that I had stayed longer at the bar near Tower Bridge that sold pints for two pounds. Truthfully, that was the primary reason for my late arrival at Hyde Park. I hadn't been ready to leave until it was dark out. The benign sunlight would have been too hostile.

So many bats. Thousands. I had no guess as to where Hyde Park's bats spent the days. Under upturned boats maybe. A whole cocoon.

Here was a couple, entering the park. I could tell that they didn't notice me. The lamplight was so weak that it barely bathed my feet in dim light. The wattage used did not encourage nighttime visitors.

This young man and young woman were the first to disrupt the quiet.

The man was walking backwards, facing the woman, just ahead of her. Though I couldn't hear their words, I could make out that they were arguing, by the tone of each of their voices—the man's hushed and attempting patience, and the woman's agitated. Why argue tonight? I thought. It was futile. The two would go home and get into bed together. No sense in arguing when you have someone.

I imagined the justification. I imagined the woman had had a dream in which the boyfriend betrayed her with her best friend as she sat watching from an opposite couch. She had not told him but had been unpleasant all day. She had been unappreciative at dinner, made jabbing comments about undercooked noodles and mushy vegetables. Now there was tension from both directions. He had betrayed her in her dreams, and she had made the day unpleasant for him. She could not come out right and blame him for his actions, but she resented that fact, and it agitated her all the more. The argument had to be about insignificant things because it could not be about bigger things such as the fact that she had dreamed of him betraying her cruelly. Although she couldn't decide if he had betrayed her or if her dreams did, she was resentful and needed to direct her resentment.

I imagined this as the argument became more audible. The man was prying, demanding to know what he did to deserve the cold silent treatment he was getting, still walking backwards. The woman felt that the man was exercising some type of power walking backwards like that, and she didn't like his confrontational posture. She pushed the man firmly in the chest, and by an awkward movement of the man, in trying to turn around and save a fall by landing on his feet, he fell to the ground, tripping over his own leg. The man fell on his side but rolled onto his back and lay flat with his arms outstretched in a hyperbolic defeated gesture. He raised his chin to his chest, but the woman was now walking back the way they had come into the park. She was obviously unsympathetic.

Three of us now in this park, all alone now. I imagined myself the happiest because I came alone. The two of them fighting. For what? A dream. It was so absurd. The man, still lying on the ground, reached into his pocket and pulled out a cellphone. I saw him press a few buttons and put the phone to his ear. The woman was receding from my view, but I perceived that she had stopped, as her figure continued to obscure the same amount of darkness. The man spoke in whispers on the phone. The woman turned and appeared to look at him still lying on the ground. She still did not walk. She saw her lover lying there defeated like a fallen angel.

She walked slowly over to where he lay talking on the phone. Once she came within reasonable speaking distance, the man and the woman put their phones away. She peeled him off the cement where she had left him broken.

He rose simply, lightly. The two walked off in the direction from which they'd appeared, arms around each other like lovers, both facing straight ahead of them. I watched their figures until they receded completely from my view. I sat with the bats, as darkness closed over the two of them. I was not poor. I was not lonely. Others would appear and recede in the darkness. I'd walk back to where I slept alone in a bed. I would miss no one.

THE RECRUIT
(The Flower and the Bird)

When she told me she was going to Taiwan, I had no reason to believe her. She had a big heart and probably would be unable to tell me, but she had lots of reasons to want to be away from me. It was impossible to say where she was going. Or for how long. She said a year. A popular trip might have been a drive south through the United States to Mexico. She could have already purchased a car. I had the audacity to chase her. She knew that. It would be simple to board a plane to Taiwan and roam the night markets. But she would not be so transparent and, therefore, not so easy to find.

Why? She had lots of reasons, like I said. I was never perfect. I was jealous, for one thing. I was depressed. Needy. Moody. Drunk. She was dodgy when I asked her—chalked it up to adventure and experience and ambition. We had been together for six years. Why now? Likely it had been planned all along. Monopolize the best years of my young life then disappear into oblivion, or Mexico, or some other place. I don't know what women want. They're fickle. Maybe a Mexican who can offer her the sea, or an Asian who can offer her the sun.

The six years weren't connubial bliss either. I pursued, she withdrew; she pursued, I withdrew. We found each other somewhere in the middle, fell apart, found each other again. And then apart. And then together again. Then she left. To where though?

She did call. Her telephone number matched the Taiwanese country code, but it is so easy to fake a country code with an Internet phone service. I could have called her from Botswana if I liked. You think it would have been easy to ask her, but women never give a straight answer. They'll utter something so plausible, so truthful-sounding, that it would be absurd to blindly believe.

I needed to recruit someone to accompany me on a search. I had not yet figured where to go. I thought perhaps Taiwan was the wisest option. I could ask around, check names that she'd dropped and businesses where she'd claimed to have been. It would be simple to at least confirm the fact that she'd been feeding me shit since even before she left. She liked to talk about Taiwanese culture, her Taiwanese apartment, the Taiwanese food and Taiwanese transportation and Taiwanese shops. So truthful-seeming, transparent-seeming, so goddamn plausible that I might have believed her if I'd ever encountered a woman who was not cunning, not duplicitous, not dubious or roundabout or evasive. My girl was all of those things. And quick-witted to boot. To research, imagine, create a "real" life in Taiwan was nothing for her. An afternoon.

While talking on the phone, I thought I detected a British inflection to her Mandarin. It was subtle, but it was there. It could have been a red herring though. Maybe she wanted to send me to Britain. She knew I had an ear for language. She was probably figuring I would go running all over fucking London like a madman searching for her. She'd like that. Anything to make me look foolish. I figured that she figured that Taiwan was so obvious that I would never bother searching for her there. Because to be so simple-minded and fly all the way to Taiwan would be idiotic. It would make me look stupid. Evidently, she hadn't thought that merely uncovering her bullshit would give me as much satisfaction as actually finding her.

I was on term at university, so I had plenty of time to find a companion, a sympathizer, preferably a woman because my flesh was getting lonely. I began showing up for classes. Women go in throngs, and the casual atmosphere of the classroom lends itself to striking up conversations. There are certain behaviours to avoid in the classroom in order to impress women. Pretending at ineptitude or ignorance will get you nowhere. Most women in the institution want a man who can challenge them, talking at length about cripplingly boring topics. Neither do you want to appear too bright though because then you'll end up with a particularly boring girl on a trip that could very well prove to be a strain on a nascent relationship.

When I showed up at classes, I surveyed the empty seats. I had to decide if I wanted a lock or a challenge. I would be globetrotting with this girl, remember. Fastidiousness was a no. A loudmouth was out of the question. I required a low-maintenance variety. Independent too. I didn't want a girl who was constantly reminding me of how little maintenance she required either. No one who says *I'm a "sweats" type of girl* or *I get ready faster than my guy friends.* That sort would not do. The more I thought about the type necessary, the more daunting the choosing became. She couldn't be a virgin, or the needy sort. I needed an independent girl who would sleep with me but be self-controlled enough to understand that our relationship was largely for practical purposes and must end when I found my love. Aesthetically, I needed a girl with darker hair. Shorter than me. Slim. A girl with great teeth. A smiley sort too, in order to keep my hopes high on the trip. A good complexion. No craters. I could not become over-particular, but I don't think my criteria were too discriminating. Sexual compatibility was a no-brainer. Often the best approach was to speak to a few women, and if I had a semi pressing against the front of my jeans, to take that for an auspicious sign.

My libido led me to different seats on different days. My classes had as few as fifteen people and as many as six hundred. The classes with six hundred were the most difficult. Sometimes I felt myself being led in many directions at once. On such occasions, I would find a seat between two potential candidates, but my attention was often divided. I planted a few seeds around, sweet-talked them, and waited for the right time to harvest.

Sadly, none of the candidates was proving as eager as I would have liked. They had not been my first choices. My first choice was a sweet little bird in my Holocaust class. I seated myself next to her every class, which was not always simple. There were over a hundred people, and it often required some crowd-scanning. One day I had a five-minute window before the lecture began. I didn't have as much time as I would have liked, but I began with the questions.

"Are you Jewish?" I asked.

"What?"

"Are you Jewish?"

"Do I look Jewish?"

"I'm not so sure I'm so good at identifying Jewish people. I would have probably had you as descended from some eastern European country."

"Then why'd you ask if I was Jewish?"

"It's a Holocaust class."

I was beginning to question how bright this bird actually was. She was sweet, no doubt about that. She smelled good, but not too good. She was shorter than I was. Slim. Dark hair. Clean skin. I was worrying that she might be one of those birds whose intelligence was inversely proportional to her looks.

"Are you Jewish?" she asked.

"No."

"You're in a Holocaust class...."

Quite possibly not the sharpest stone on

the earth. But I could not ignore my semi. And ultimately it was judge and jury in this choice I had to make. She looked at me like she was confused. I was doing my best not to condescend.

"So was I right that you're of eastern European descent?" I asked.

"Technically, you thought I was Jewish first."

"No. I asked if you were Jewish. I guessed you were European."

"I'm not sure this is an appropriate discussion to be having in a Holocaust class."

"Lithuanian? You're Lithuanian, right?"

"..."

"You could also pass for a Scandinavian."

"I'm Czech."

"I was close."

I smiled at her. The lecture began. The merciless ethnic cleansing of millions doesn't often put girls in the mood to swoon. I had to be delicate. The situation required a great deal of tact and sensitivity on my part. I had to appear engaged, wholly attentive to the lecture. Latent guilt can make the most reluctant scholars learn. I conceived several off-the-cuff witticisms as we were discussing *Night*, but the time was inopportune to showcase a sense of humour. I felt that my imagined comments would penetrate the steeliest exterior of a girl, would woo this little bird under any other circumstances. I required a change of venue to train this bird to drink from my hand. I thought about waiting for some kind of divine intervention or serendipity, but then I bucked at the thought, as the classroom was a godless place. I would have to seize the day and not idly let time pass. My little flower could be speeding away in a car, farther from me by the minute.

As I was leaving class, I engaged the little bird in conversation. The aisles were crowded and were emptying like a movie theatre. We were near the back, so I had time to get sufficiently into a conversation. As we left the auditorium and the building, we stepped into a light rain, and we came to a fork in one of the many paths that ran through campus. I gleaned from her body language the direction she was going in and altered my own language so it would become evident that I was going that way too.

To shield herself from the rain, this little bird was holding the hood of her sweatshirt above her head with thumb and forefinger, making a beak so the rain wouldn't wet her hair. The gesture endeared her to me, as I suspected that her morning routine included straightening her hair, and to get it wet would undo her labour. She did not want her hair to go poofy on her. Perhaps she was particularly conscious of her hair because I was there. A good sign. She could be hot for me. She would not remind me how low-maintenance she was. But her moderate makeup and subtle scent placed her somewhere in the middle of the maintenance scale. I also judged her hair, a jet black, to be her natural colour. If we were travelling together, she would not need a separate bag for cosmetics; she could manage simply with one large piece of luggage. What concerned me was her small frame. She needed to be able to carry forty-plus pounds on her back without annoying pleas to stop whenever we covered a substantial distance by foot.

We walked into a campus building with a Tim Hortons. I asked her if she had time for coffee. She did. This pleased me, the fact that she drank coffee. On our chase, we would be able to consult maps and do much of the thinking at coffee shops. We would outline potential locations of my flower.

I allowed her to order first and let her pay for her own coffee. A long trip would prove too costly for me to provide for both of us. I had inheritance money enough from my father to cover my own expenses on the trip. I could likely cover her as well, but the duration of the thing was impossible to know, and so it would have been unwise for me to give this bird the impression that she would be wined and dined. If the search went smoothly in the sense that I located my flower without too much globetrotting, I might provide the little bird with a kind of bonus, say a flight home for her efforts. This is assuming that my flower would see that I was not fully squandered just yet, that I was her own, her lovely partner, and that we would come together again under a brand new sun.

There were no seats at the Tim Hortons, but I knew of one Tim Hortons on campus that always had empty seats. We took an underground passageway between the campus buildings so we wouldn't get wet. We chattered as we walked, about superficial things, and I desired to tell her about the trip and the chase and my flower and where she came into it, but it was still not time. The passageway was dim and gaudily painted, and it echoed. I wondered if she knew of this subterranean passage. Maybe she thought I was knowledgeable and worldly because I knew of the tunnel.

As I had presumed, the other Tim Hortons was mostly empty, so we settled in by a window.

"I like your hair," I said. "Is it dyed?"

"No."

"But you straighten it in the morning?"

"Can you tell?"

"Yes. Impressed?"

"Very."

"So your hair is undyed but straightened...."

"That's right."

"Very nice."

Though she had been only confirming my thoughts so far, all this was very important to know unambiguously.

"So, in terms of makeup, supposing you were to travel.... You don't wear much, do you?"

"Wow. You know how to make someone self-conscious."

"I don't mean like that. What I mean is, suppose you were going somewhere, suppose the place were overseas someplace, like in Asia, would you carry a separate bag for cosmetics?"

"Of course not. That's ridiculous."

"Isn't it? That's what I would have guessed. You'd bring a hair straightener though?"

"It depends how long I was going for...."

"Suppose you had no idea how long you were going for."

"Well, then I suppose I would probably bring one."

"Right. That's reasonable."

We talked some more, mostly about superficial things without real weight—religion, school, work, books. I kept trying to steer the conversation towards more practical matters, but it was proving difficult. At one point, however, the little bird was talking about her ennui with scholarship and work, and I took that opportunity to test the waters.

"Come to Tahiti with me," I said. It sounded somehow better, sunnier, than Taiwan with its typhoons and monsoons, or dreary England, or wherever we might need to go. At this point, it was not necessarily an untruth. After all, we might end up having to go to Tahiti.

"That'd be nice," she said.

"Really. Come to Tahiti. Let's take a trip."

She looked confoundedly at me. "I'm in the middle of a school term. And so are you. Plus there's the even more glaring issue of hardly knowing each other."

"See, but you're all hung up about time. There's all the time in the world in Bora-Bora."

"It sounds nice. It would be amazing to get away from the cold. And school."

"It's easier than you think. What would you say if I said I already bought you a non-refundable ticket to Tahiti?"

"I would probably say that's impossible on account of your not knowing me before today. I would probably also say that's insane."

"Right. Well, I don't have a non-refundable ticket to Tahiti. But why don't we do it?"

"I'd love to. Really. I just can't."

"Sure you can," I said. "It's easy. You just have to say yes, and I'll take care of the rest. It's as easy as that. You say yes and pack a bag. That's it. Just say yes." I heard myself breaking my own rules about not wining and dining and spending, but I felt like I was making some headway.

"You're actually serious right now, aren't you?"

"Completely serious."

"You're insane," she said.

"Not really, no. Just say the word. It's easy. I hardly know you, and I already know about your shitty job at a shitty motel, how badly school sucks.... I understand. You're what? Twenty years old? Twenty-one maybe? You're not always gonna be able to just get up and go wherever the hell you want to with some guy you just met. People will judge you and throw a straightjacket on you, but we've got a chance now. Do you see this? Do you understand?"

"I don't know.... I'd be crazy to do it. I hardly know you."

"I hardly know you either. For all I know, you have severed heads sitting in jars full of brine in your refrigerator, but I'm willing to risk it. I'd be crazy for going with you, too."

"Well, you're definitely nuts. I can tell that already."

"Say it. Say yes."

"I can't."

"Why not?"

"I don't know. I just can't."

"You don't like me."

"No, it's not that. I don't know you."

"You will. There's time."

"Well then, all in due time."

She made me work for it. There were coffees and drinks and even a couple meals. She started to bend though. And one evening, after a particularly inspired speech by yours truly re: doing something totally uncharacteristic and unordinary but something that, regardless of outcome, like whether it turns out wonderful and life-changing or terrible and life-changing, is almost impossible to regret, I really emphasized the mundanity of the future, the everydayness, and how, assuming I wasn't some homicidal psycho (which she intuited that I wasn't by this point), it really would be a missed opportunity were she to discard the idea. Maybe it was because we had already finished a bottle of red wine and she was feeling inspired or filled with spontaneity, or maybe she just felt worn out with her life, or who knows why? But she consented. I was probably as surprised as she was, but I told her I'd hold her to her word, and she didn't retreat.

I had no intention of going to Tahiti, in fact never have, but it had a remoteness and romanticism to it that Taiwan might not have had. The little bird took the bait too. I had not yet apprised her of the purpose of the vacation either. All in due time, as she might've said. Somewhere in my mind I thought it might be prudent to simply leave her in the dark. It would come to light in time, and I needed to get to know her better before revealing too much and running the risk of shooting myself in the foot, so to speak.

My focus and fixity started paying off. I was able to let my place for the rest of the lease. I got my tuition money back. The little bird had set about doing the same things, all the while telling me, or herself, that she must be crazy. We saw more and more of each other through the preparatory stages. Neither of us had much on our plate since she quit her job and we withdrew from school, and we had about a week of leisure until the flight. She still didn't know that we were going to Taiwan, and as our departure grew nearer, telling her became no less daunting.

We hadn't slept together either. One night when we were out at the pharmacy, picking up miniature shampoos and toothpastes and other miniature travel-friendly items, I suggested we try on the old glove, so to speak, to see if it fits. The little bird thought this rather unromantic, the way I approached the topic in a practical manner, which was my MO, but I nonetheless understood her position and told her to consider what I'd said withdrawn and then proceeded to go about it the right way.

We were in her living room, watching TV, and I poured us some wine. I poured hers to the edge so that she could not realistically lift the glass to her lips without spilling. Not even the steady hands of a surgeon could have. She had to sip her first few sips before it was possible. We drank two bottles of the cheap red before I got around to broaching the topic of sex again. I was brash now. I had tiptoed the first time and done it unromantically. I know what girls like to hear. Either sugary come-ons or vulgar honesty. Whether they admit it or not.

"You look gorgeous," I said.

"Thanks." She was drunk and coy.

"I'd like to do awful things to you."

"Like what? What do you want to do to me?"

"Enough of this pussyfooting," I said, taking charge. "Let's go to your bedroom."

"See? That wasn't so hard."

It was kind of sloppy in the bedroom. You could tell it was unscripted and we'd been drinking. I took her sweatshirt off, and she had on another shirt underneath. And if you'd believe it, she had on an even-other one, a spaghetti-strapped one, under that. They were getting progressively tighter, and the second one was a T-shirt, which I caught on her head, and trying impatiently to get it off, grabbing at the bottom of the shirt, which I was struggling with above her head, I managed to knock her off balance into the wall. She had trouble with my belt after that, on account of her trying to undo it with her teeth. It was this double-pronged variety that was not so easy to undo.

I had a semi from the whole undressing process, and when I finally threw her on the bed naked, things unfolded much less gracelessly. She was easy to move with my hands. We rolled around, one over the other, kissing. I kissed her face, her neck, her body. When I entered her, her vagina was sopping wet. Neither of us had the foresight to discuss condoms, but when I was about to finish, I told her so, and she scanned the room quickly and told me to cum in the garbage can.

"The garbage can?" I said. But by that time, there was no time, and instead of coming on her sheets, I lunged forward and came on her torso.

"I didn't want to get it all over your sheets," I said.

"Thanks." A note of sarcasm. She was kinda holding her arms out like she didn't want to touch the ejaculate on her. She asked me to grab a dirty piece of laundry from her closet to mop it up. She cleaned up, and since she hadn't finished, I fingered her until she came—just before my hand got so tired that I would have had to stop. When she finished, she worked her way under my arm and had her face almost in my armpit. She looked tired.

I said, "Listen, I know this sucks, but I couldn't get tickets to Tahiti."

"What?" she said sleepily, waking a little. "You told me we had booked already."

"I did book. But we're not going to Tahiti; we're going to Taiwan."

"Why Taiwan?"

"Well, alphabetically, it was about as close as I could get."

"Taiwan, huh...?"

"Yes. I promise it'll be good there."

"I've never been to Asia. We can always go to Tahiti next time."

"Sure," I said. "Next time."

She fell asleep. She really was a knockout. Her black hair was splayed all over my chest, and it was scratchy, but I didn't want to disturb her, so I laid still. She had a delicate little upturned nose and white-white skin. Most women with skin that white tend to be blotchy, but hers was creamy soft. Unblemished. I did a good job picking this one out, I thought. A great choice. A bargain. Look at her: so peaceful it was making me tired. I wanted to be wherever she was right then. If only I could meet her in sleep. It consoled me to know that she'd be there again in the morning though. I fell asleep simply.

Less than a week later, my little bird and I were at the airport. We had checked our bags and were through the terminal, into the gate, waiting to board. I was having a particularly difficult time understanding the change in time.

"So it's twelve hours ahead there," I said. "We lose all the time we're on the plane, plus the twelve hours changing time zones. But what if someone were perpetually flying east, only ever landing to refuel? Wouldn't the days be going by almost twice as fast? And going west. If you just flew continually west, couldn't time slow right down to a crawl? Like you could get an aircraft equivalent of a houseboat and live up there and you'd be passing almost no time at all?"

I started drawing on a receipt, writing down the lengths of flights and the relative time in different cities at each point, attempting to make it simple, but the only conclusion I reached was that I would never understand jumping time zones perpetually in one direction.

We boarded when the speaker announced our row, and we were against the side of the plane. I sat at the window, and she the aisle.

There were two columns of seats, an aisle, three more columns, another aisle, then another two columns. So we sat in relative privacy. We shared a set of headphones and watched an awful movie, during which she fell asleep in the nook of my arm. She was getting comfortable there in the nook of my arm. I was learning to take extra care that my armpits were washed and deodorized to accommodate her. I kind of had to go to the bathroom, but I hadn't the heart to wake her, or to try and extract her head from under my arm. I let her sleep, and I eventually fell off too.

When she woke, I had already been awake for a bit, my urge to pee mysteriously quelled. I pressed the button for one of the flight attendants and ordered us a couple plastic cups of red wine.

"So, Taiwan?" she said, holding up her cup. "This is crazy. This whole trip is crazy."

"Too late to second-guess now. I've already hooked you on, line and sinker."

"I don't think that's the expression."

We cheers'd our cups—it was unsatisfying on account of the plastic—and had a drink. I had my one arm around her still, and I felt good. I had had little touch with my flower before leaving. I mentioned nothing about dropping out of school, or letting my place, or taking a trip, or anything at all about my little bird. I hadn't mentioned it much to anyone, as I had no one to answer to and no one who would have really cared anyhow. Since dropping out of school and while planning the trip, I had been sleeping more soundly. Even there on the plane, I felt right. The little bird was right. What we were doing, I decided, was the thing to do.

We had a couple more drinks on the plane, and my little bird was already a bit flushed by the time we arrived. Then, stepping out into the thick humidity of Taipei, we both remarked on our heaviness. With the added weight of our backpacks and the restlessness of being so long in the air, we were both pretty well floored and decided that before we set about doing anything at all, we would need to find a room and sleep.

We caught a cab to a hostel somewhere near the heart of Taipei, and we had exchanged a fair bit of currency and found that our NT, with the exchange rate taken into account, would give us plenty of mileage. We got a room with a double bed, and my little bird, liking this hostel at least as much as the next one, neatly unpacked her bag, settling in for a while. I had bought a pack of cigarettes from the shop next to the hostel and smoked one by the open window.

"Taipei," I said.

"I can't believe I'm here, we're here," she said.

She finished organizing her travel stuffs, and I met her in bed. We stripped down to our underwear and hopped under a thin sheet on the double bed.

"It's early to say," she said, "but this might not be crazy. This might be right."

She kissed me on the mouth and settled in under my arm and fell asleep. Again, I must have been downwind of the melatonin she gave off—and certainly there must have been something chemical about it—for I hardly remembered seeing her peaceful puckered sleeping-face.

My little bird and I spent a few days visiting mosques, riding the MRT, and wandering night markets. Like me, she was thrilled whenever she recalled the exchange of our dollar for the NT. We didn't worry about spending a couple hundred NT on dinner. There was no need for frugality. We went to KTV places and performed karaoke. We took a two-day trip to the beach in Keelung. We lay in the sun. My little bird had on this navy two-piece that drove me crazy. We fucked like animals at our hotel. I felt like royalty. Taiwanese people were coming up to us and asking if they could take our picture. I knew it was on account of my little bird, who looked brilliant in her swimsuit. She was sheepish, but I convinced her that no one would ever see these photos. The Taiwanese were evidently charmed by her, and I couldn't blame them a bit. I had no problems showing her off. The more people who saw, the better. I felt that I would be cropped out of the photos later.

We returned to Taipei one evening. I told her that I wanted to do some exploring on my own.

"That's fine," she said. "I'm tired anyhow. I'm just gonna hang out at the hostel."

I wandered off towards a night market. I began thinking of my flower, my raison d'être. She might be here, I thought. She could be anywhere. She could be here or she could be in England. She could be in England or just as easily in Mexico.

There were stalls set up all around the night market. A lot of fragrant food was being prepared, but I was not hungry. I browsed the stalls all around. I was looking at a stall selling jewellery when a piece with a jade gemstone caught my eye. My little flower had always loved jade. She would have liked it. If I were to find her and show up with this necklace with the jade gemstone, everything would be absolutely fine. She would see me and the jade gemstone, and she would welcome me in, and we would be fine. She would tell me that I was her only, had always been her very own only, and we would be together. I held the necklace, and it was a fine necklace indeed. I told the owner of the merchandise to hold onto it for me, but he understood no English.

I continued browsing. I found a string of cultured golden pearls. I thought of my little bird lying down in bed at the hostel. Her white skin growing more tan. Her wide-eyed presence and capriciousness. It's crazy, she was always saying. And also, I can't believe I came, I can't believe I'm here, I must really be out of my mind. These pearls would look good on her, I knew. It didn't say how much they cost, but I had not yet encountered a price that seemed exorbitant. How much could they be? I wondered. And then deciding that they could not cost too much, for nothing was too much, I handed them over to the gentleman running the counter and opened my wallet.

GRADUATION

The lobby was a congregation of strapping upright future successes. I did not consider myself one of them. The girl standing in front of me looked ravishing in her shiny silver dress. I imagined that she had done interesting things and was manoeuvring her way quickly up through the lower rungs to the top of some ladder. I told her that I felt absurd wearing a too-big black rental gown that cost me twenty-five bucks. She smiled a toothy smile—too many teeth, I decided. I would not be able to sex her on account of her teeth. Also, she was about my height and therefore much too tall. She would look into my eyes while I was sexing her. There was something slightly cockeyed about her too.

I was right, though, about the interesting things. She had lived with native Africans in a hut, working for a not-for-profit organization, building schools or feeding the famished or immunizing the at-risk. I got all this in the first two minutes of chatter. She was involved with commendable organizations that helped the derelict and the underprivileged. Her life was just ducky. She said she felt a little absurd wearing the ceremonial gown too, but I could tell that it wasn't true.

In the rows of folding chairs, I volunteered my assessment of the uninspiring commencement speech to my neighbours. The man had his name on a series of textbooks—heavy, daunting, lifeless ones that I hoped to never see again. His gown was iridescent, even more ridiculous than my rental.

After a needlessly long period of waiting, a brief and untriumphant walk across the stage where I knelt before the Chancellor as he took the sash from my arm and laid it around my neck like a loose noose, and I answered truly "I don't know" to his inquiry about my future plans, the ceremony ended. I spoke with the girl in the silver dress for a few moments in the lobby. Though I didn't want to have sex with her, the ceremony had made me feel lonely and cheap, so I entertained the idea again. I returned my gown with uncalled-for immediacy and went outside into the day. I sat on the grass and smoked a cigarette. Graduates posed for photographs with their friends and families. Crowds of students who evidently knew each other laughed and smiled.

Over the course of a few beers at the on-campus bar, I made conversation with people who looked unoccupied. I spoke about my graduation to the bartender. I wondered aloud why there weren't more people celebrating. Where were the drunken revellers? I scanned the bar for these people. Finding none, I left, telling the bartender to keep my stool warm.

I strolled around campus. The only building I cared to go into was the library, but it was under construction for the summer. I smoked on a bench in front of the library, where years earlier I had weepily finished reading *Frankenstein* late one night after the library had closed, as the rain soaked me through and dog-eared the pages of the book. I remembered looking out the ninth-floor windows from the study booths. I remembered dreaming, believing in things.

By the end of the cigarette, I needed to use a washroom. After a hot beer shit, I looked at my freshly shaven face in the mirror, washed my hands more thoroughly than necessary, and walked back outside without knowing where to go. I meandered around most of the campus with vague notions such as how I might run into some girl I had known tangentially but not too well, and that we would exchange hardly a word but search madly for a discreet place to have sex, and that, finding none, we would strip down and fuck like animals in the bushes. I tried to believe this could happen.

I wandered back to the bar for a couple more Canadians as another ceremony dragged on. I was less talkative this time around. I slumped on the stool and imagined that the waitress with runs in her stockings would drag me into the kitchen and fuck me on the vegetable counter. I was beginning to feel drunk.

My friend finally called. I drank the rest of my beer in one pull and walked out to find that the sun had reached the point, or rather I had reached the point, where it was very nearly hostile. I had ditched my grey sports coat. My white shirt was untucked with the top few buttons undone. My tie hung loosely around my neck.

My friend Rich and I walked north along the road circumscribing the campus, suitably dubbed Ring Road. We walked past our first-year residence building, and past Mission Hill, where we had spent much of the first week of university smoking joints in the shadowy pines, and past our former residence's cafeteria, where I had put on an impressive twenty-five pounds in under eight months eating mostly club sandwiches and spicy chicken wraps, and past the on-campus Tim Hortons where I had worked a brief stint before my employer and I decided I wasn't right for the position, and past the bushes where we had uncovered a beaten-down shack, and past the boards for the outdoor rink where I used to play pickup hockey in the winter, and past the swimming pool where the mustachioed middle-aged man had ogled me in the shower, and past the field where we had played orientation games, all bright-eyed and eager to know each other.

"Thank the gods it's over," I said.

"Big wank," Rich agreed.

We found Rich's car in the congested parking lot across the street from campus. I lit a cigarette and put on some sad music. We hit the main street and gathered a little speed, and I felt the whole damned city drawing up close behind us.

BODY LANGUAGE

Jesse met Jordan at Sid's party that Sid was throwing above all else to be liked. Sid didn't really feel much one way or the other about either Jesse or Jordan but invited them all the same, hoping that they would like him. Sid rarely thought about Jesse or Jordan at all but bcc'd them the email invitation, and Jesse and Jordan showed up, perhaps an indication that Jesse and Jordan quite liked Sid, Sid thought.

Jesse and Jordan struck up a conversation around a knee-high coffee table in the living room, and it, that is to say the nascent conversation, began as they were on opposite sides of this table, and Jesse was uncertain whether or not he should walk around so that the knee-high table wouldn't impede a more intimate conversation by occupying all that physical space between them, but Jesse hesitated because it was a bold gesture indeed to slyly walk around the table while maintaining the conversation that he judged—though he was never certain about these things—was going swimmingly and progressing to a point of intimacy that might get stifled by this table occupying all this physical space between them. Jesse didn't want to unnerve Jordan, who at this point in time was trying to project her "interested" face, which indeed she was, that is to say interested, but it was not enough to be interested, *I must* convey *that interest*, Jordan thought, and the only mirror for Jordan to check her interested face in was at an oblique angle to her and would necessitate a break in the conversation, thereby producing the exact opposite of the desired effect of apparent interestedness.

It appeared to Jesse that Jordan was not looking him quite in the eye, that Jordan in fact had her glance fixed just slightly above and between his eyes, and Jesse wondered if there was something unusual on his forehead, perspiration say, but Jesse had no mirror to consult without giving himself away and so bit his lip about the whole thing, but not actually, of course, because Jesse wanted nothing less than to look nervous. Jordan was silently thinking contemptuous thoughts about herself, regarding her inability to maintain eye contact, especially now with Jesse, whom Jordan wanted so badly to meet eyes with, but Jordan being bashful and all was unable and stared rather obtusely just above Jesse's eyes, a trick she had learned from public speaking that she, at this moment in time, wished she had never learned.

"I think the same thing," Jesse was saying, hoping to be liked.

"I'm so glad," Jordan responded, beaming, desperate to appear sincere, which she was.

Jesse fixed his glance on Jordan—who was looking obliquely at his face still—trying to, like, pierce through Jordan's eyes to her mind's eye and say but not say, convey, *I like you, Jordan, boy do I, but do you like me?* trying to collude looks of desire and inquisition just like that, and Jordan was thinking that perhaps Jesse really had to go to the washroom, as Jesse's face kept contorting, sending really rather mixed signals. Jordan, now confused, suddenly feeling as though she had cornered Jesse into conversation; Jesse, who very well might be wanting, no, *needing*, to go to the washroom but perhaps was too sheepish to say so; or even worse, Jesse might have just felt trapped and so was projecting this face that was communicating, *I need to go to the washroom*, when all Jesse really wanted was to get away from Jordan, and Jordan felt just like Jesse had torn her heart out and was chewing on it.

"Do you need to go to the washroom?" Jordan asked.

"Um...no," Jesse responded, wondering if Jordan was intimating that in fact she had to go to the washroom, which sometimes, Jesse knew, people did—like ask questions only as a guise for what they actually wanted/needed to do, like when someone asks, *Do you want to eat that?* they're really saying, *I want to eat that*, and Jesse suspected that Jordan maybe needed to go to the washroom.

"Do *you* need to go to the washroom?" Jesse asked.

"Um, what? Uh, no," Jordan responded,

somewhat perplexed and thinking, *Have I been holding my genitalia? Are my legs turned in imperceptibly at the knees? Could I smell like urine?* and Jordan had a strong impulse to sniff her armpits for that ammonia smell, but she could tell in her lateral vision, as she stared at Jesse's forehead, that Jesse was looking at her, and so did nothing, and it seemed to Jordan as though one of them maybe should say something again.

Jesse and Jordan stood, still, with a knee-high table between them still, looking dumbly at each other's eyes and foreheads, occasionally squinting in order to better read the other person, and because of their involvement in this inquisitive stare-down, their conversation had fizzled into quietude, which contributed to an impression, to anyone aloof of the situation, that Jesse and Jordan were preparing to, like, draw guns from their holsters.

Jesse, feeling the weight of every silent moment, stood dumb, and it appeared to Jesse that Jordan kept opening her mouth to say something but continually checked herself, and Jesse believed this inability to squeeze the words through her mouth was an indication that Jordan wanted to say something really difficult to say, such as, *I think we should mingle with other people, as right now you're monopolizing my time and inhibiting me from really getting to know these other individuals who look, each one individually, somehow more interesting than you,* and Jordan thought that Jesse's silent contemplation was his thoughtful attempt to devise a way to sever the conversation, and she could not help herself but absolutely had to say:

"Was there something you wanted to say?"

Jesse wondered if once again Jordan was projecting her desire to say something by asking him what *he* wanted to say, but Jesse realized that he already repeated her washroom question and could not now repeat this same question, though he would have liked to.

"Not really.... Good party, isn't it?" Jesse said, and immediately thought that Jordan must misconstrue this comment through no fault of her own filtering, or percolating, thought processes, where asinine comments like his own trickle down and are exposed as pure little droplets of *intention*, because Jesse knew that Jordan knew he was not in fact talking about the party when he was talking about the party, so Jordan would have to inevitably conclude that Jesse was either a) forcefully hitting on her, or b) just about the most pathetic and socially inept individual she has ever engaged with in conversation at a party.

"Yes. It was awfully nice to get an invitation. I don't even really know the host that well," Jordan said.

"Me neither," Jesse chimed, and Jordan was glad that Jesse didn't know Sid well, because she thought Sid rather a rodent, that is, sneaky and insincere, and Jesse thought much the same thing, and both Jesse and Jordan had attended the party solely because they were, individually and respectively, in fact quite lonely, in spite of the fact that their mothers, respectively, have told them, each, that they are incredibly unique and lovely people, and both Jesse and Jordan, in their heart of hearts, are inclined to believe that their mothers are sound in judgment.

Jesse felt suddenly united with Jordan, neither of them knowing Sid very well, in his case not knowing anyone here very well (which, unbeknownst to him, was the case for Jordan as well), and this conversation, truth be told, was the most engaging and thrilling conversation Jesse has had since he can remember. Jordan thought that Jesse was someone she would truly like to get to know, he seemed so *himself*, and Jordan was caught between a throbbing desire for Jesse and a longing desire *to be like* Jesse in his himselfness. Jordan figured that Jesse must have exponentially more conversations with the opposite gender than she did, because he was so *collected*, like together and himself, when she had all these feelings that defy description and suggestion running through her blood and her bones so that they just might burst right through the surface of her skin.

Jordan, feeling an urgent desire to get herself together, both figuratively and literally, needed a moment alone in the washroom, and there she would be able to do both the figurative getting-together, that is subdue and channel her fractionized energies and really work in one direction and be able to, like, wow Jesse, which she felt she hadn't been in a position to do so far, being everywhere and nowhere at one and the same time, and also the literal getting-together, that is accentuate the desirable features on her face with a touch of makeup here and/or there (and desirable facial features, Jesse thought, Jordan had in plenitude).

"Will you excuse me?" Jordan asked. "I need to visit the little girl's room."

"Of course. By all means," Jesse responded.

Jordan left to the washroom, and Jesse wondered what he had been thinking with regard to that "by all means," as though suggesting Jordan would need all her means to go to the washroom, and Jesse thought it profoundly stupid what he had said, and he retrieved a drink and sat down on the corner cushion of the couch, steeping/stewing in his profound stupidity and ineptness. Meanwhile, Jordan expertly accentuated her high cheekbones and curled her beautiful and much-coveted long lashes in front of the mirror, thinking it was just an awful phrase to use, that "little girl's room," and she imagined Jesse would have fled the party by the time she got out of the washroom, and she thought that it was a clear indication of her scatterbrainedness that she had had to excuse herself when everything had been so engrossing/natural/perfect. She felt she always ruined these moments, like when she knew she was supposed to say or do something to create a *moment* in her life, like really consummate it, and knowing full well what it would take in a situation to have one of these real moments, like as in, say, a book, Jordan still inevitably ended up saying or doing the wrong thing.

Jesse anxiously kept one eye on the hallway down which Jordan had disappeared, permanently perhaps, given that there might have been a window through which Jordan, with her slender figure, would wedge in order not to have to meet his sad eyes ever again. Jordan strode, *tiptoed*, she felt, down the hallway and paused right before she would see the knee-high coffee table in the living room so she could truly *gather* herself before, she hoped, resuming a beautiful/perfect conversation with Jesse, who, she prayed, would still be standing quite alone in the position where she had left him.

Turning the corner, Jordan didn't see Jesse standing, and her heart just about exploded, no, *imploded*, tinily, as it might if she had to witness a dog getting squished by a pickup truck or as when she sees a slim man pulling a weightier man in a rickshaw through narrow streets. Only moments later, *years*, Jordan thought, she witnessed Jesse sitting alone on the corner of the couch, and now her heart, which had imploded, exploded back to a size that was, like, slightly bigger than it was even before she came to the party and first engaged in conversation with Jesse.

Jesse witnessed Jordan walking as Jordan witnessed Jesse sitting, and the swelling of hearts was absolutely tangible, or *palpable*, to anyone in the vicinity. Jordan wondered why Jesse had sat down—perhaps it was so not to be espied by her upon her return—and she did not want to immediately go and sit, so audacious and suggestive as it would have been, directly next to Jesse. Jesse saw Jordan circling around, much like, he thought, a negatively polarized magnet to another negatively polarized magnet, but in fact, as anyone aloof would have noticed, it was more like a moth to a flame, or a spider circling the prey caught in her web, like you knew Jordan was going to get there, but Jesse didn't.

Jordan came up nonchalantly, clumsily, she thought, and sat down on the other corner cushion, leaving a middle cushion between them and looking straight ahead, like not over at Jesse. Jesse looked over at her, and he felt that Jordan, having left the middle cushion un-sat-on, did not wish to engage in conversation anymore but sat there more out of either default, it being one of the only seats to sit in, or respect, like respecting the fact that they *had* engaged in conversation and acknowledging that she in fact knew him even if she didn't feel like speaking presently.

Why hasn't he said anything to me? Jordan thought, feeling completely idiotic having dolled herself up and collected herself in the washroom for Jesse. *He thinks I'm repulsive*, Jordan thought, and she sat there, too depressed to actually move her limbs, let alone hoist herself up with the arm of the couch and leave, so she sat for what felt to Jordan like longer than her life leading up to the moment when she sat down on the couch, until she heard Jesse's voice:

"Hey." It was a voice of, like, real butter-scotch.

"Oh.... Hey," Jordan said warmly, warmly enough, she hoped.

Jesse and Jordan resumed their engrossing/beautiful/perfect conversation, and the dwindling crowd paid them no mind, but Jesse and Jordan were keenly aware of the fact that they must be leaving, but neither dared move a muscle, aside from the minimum usage required to move your mouth, blink, smile. *This has to end*, Jordan thought gloomily, and Jesse, feeling the pangs of time with each person exiting, thought dolefully, *This can't go on forever*.

"Well..." Jesse said, it now being beyond the level of intimacy at the party where Jesse was comfortable being there, not particularly liking, or even *knowing*, the host.

"I suppose we should get going," Jordan said, immediately wishing she could have simply said, *Let's never leave; we'll disregard the smarmy host and live here.*

"Yes. That's what I was thinking," Jesse said.

Jesse and Jordan grabbed their coats off the stiff coat rack, saying goodnight to their host, each pledging to call Sid and each not really meaning it, and they walked out into the crisp night and stood on the sidewalk, silently, pretending to observe the moon and the stars, pretending to be too rapt to hail one of the empty cabs driving by, both thinking that this is where it ends.

"I'll hail you a cab," Jesse said.

Jesse thought it would be chivalrous of him to hail Jordan a cab, and he stepped a foot into the street, got his hailing hand out, and hailed the next empty cab that drove by. The cab pulled up to the curb, and Jesse and Jordan looked at each other longingly, neither of them recognizing longing in the other, and they timorously held hands facing each other, Jesse's right with Jordan's left and Jordan's right with Jesse's left, locked like oppositely polarized magnets, and Jesse bent in, not even believing that he failed to stifle the impulse, and kissed Jordan on the cheek.

"Goodnight," Jesse said.

"It was great meeting you," Jordan said, getting into the cab now, leaving forever to live in some beautiful and harmonious world that Jesse would never be allowed to be a part of.

"You too," Jesse said, the words squeezing through the cab door just before it closed, and Jesse watched the cab pull off into the night and then walked home.

Jesse got home swiftly, and he crawled into bed, cursing his ineptness, his clumsiness, his reservedness. Jesse replayed his blunders like a slideshow: every social ineptitude, every impotence and incompetence, until the memories suddenly evoked Jordan's beautiful face in his mind, blanketing everything else. Jordan had arrived home and poured herself a glass of water and got in bed, thinking about Jesse. *I didn't even get his phone number, or even his last name*, Jordan thought, reproving herself and her stupidity and her ugly timidity. Jordan lay awake thinking of Jesse, how exactly himself

and beautiful and sincere he was, and the two
of them, unaware for now and forever what
the other is doing/thinking, touch themselves
thinking of the other, as hands work, calves
flex, toes point, pores flow, hearts throb.

AFTER THE SILENCE

To say it wasn't going great would be to put it lightly. We hadn't been carnal in two weeks and pretty much stopped speaking to each other about a week ago. Lily was going for beers after work every day like a Brit, which wasn't like her. A lot of effort on both sides goes into not speaking to someone you live with, especially in close quarters. The apartment was essentially one big room with a few extra turns and corners, so to refrain from speaking, you needed to pretend to be occupied at all times. Even when you stare at the wall, you have to do it with purpose, as though you're waiting for the wall to open up and reveal something. There was no TV, which makes a situation like this more difficult. If someone were to view us aloofly, together in that tiny apartment, they'd think we were philosophers of some sort, gazing here and there with intent eyes, with meaning.

I was contemplating all this with a closed book in front of me as the barista brought me my espresso drink. She was the barista I liked. With things going so bad with Lily, I couldn't even think about bedding another girl. That's the way it is with me. If I'm getting mine, I can think about bedding girls who would currently disgust me. Right now I look at women and see more problems. I can only manage to place women in the same position as the woman in my life, who assumes the role of the representative of all women. Every woman appears a problem. I picture each of them sitting across the room from me with an idiotic glazed expression on her face, contorted in an attempt to mean deep contemplation.

I thanked the barista sarcastically, thinking about how miserable she'd probably make me if given the opportunity. I watched her serve customers and thought about her strangling cats in alleyways on her walk home. The coffee was hot, but it tasted like someone in back was grinding the beans with the soles of their boots. I left about half the coffee on the table with some change and took off.

I went home, and Lily was there. I'd taken to sneaking into the apartment, trying to catch Lily doing absolutely nothing so that she would have no other out but to engage me in conversation. When I crept around the corner, Lily was there on the couch, but she was reading a magazine. Magazines, unlike novels, make it difficult to appear engaged. I knew she wasn't reading an article, but she was careful not to turn the pages too quickly, as everyone does when they know they're being watched as they read a magazine. It's like if you sent a person into an art gallery by himself. He'd walk straight through the middle of the room, gaze about him, move on, and say, "So what?" But there are always other people there, so people stroke their tuft of chest hair, or remove and replace their glasses as though they were a magnifying glass or 3-D glasses. So many pursed lips, skyward-cast eyes, and hands behind backs at art galleries, it's enough to make you sick. I had a thought to run right to Lily's magazine and catch her stuck on a page totally without text. I left that thought alone.

"I don't feel loved," Lily said.

Those were the first words she addressed to me in days.

"You ain't the only one," I said.

"I mean before this. Before the silence. I thought I'd at least tell you that I'm moving out now."

"Where are you going?" I asked.

"I found a place."

"Well, what the fuck am I supposed to do?"

"You'll be fine," she said.

"The first time you speak in fucking weeks," I said. "Fucking fantastic."

"Did you think one of us would start speaking again and everything would be on the mend?" she said. "It doesn't work like that."

"You don't feel loved," I said. "That's funny. You haven't looked at me in weeks or touched me in longer. Loved. That's funny."

"It's just not the right time," she said. "I didn't plan this."

"That's nice to know," I said. "I woulda said you did a piss-poor job if you did."

"Henry," she said.

That was the end of the conversation. With it came one of those looks combining sadness and pity and frustration and pain and regret, one of those looks that makes you search for the nearest window only to struggle with whether to jump yourself or defenestrate your loved one like a piece of rotten fruit.

Since there was nothing else to discuss, we returned to silence and avoided eye contact. I ate a piece of baguette for dinner and sat on the couch opposite Lily, drinking cheap red wine from a coffee mug. I spent the evening watching red wine spill down the neck of the bottle like spider legs. I slept on the couch, and Lily in the bed. I know what you're thinking. Shouldn't I have gotten the bed? Probably. Maybe. Yes. I'm yellow like that though. I let people shit on me and then clean it up myself. It's a terrible thing to be spineless, but I truly didn't care where I slept.

Lily was gone when I woke up. I went to my job putting up posters for a TESOL program. That is actually a job. They didn't even really monitor me. I ballparked how many hours I spent doing it, and they paid me. I had been doing it for a few weeks. People would just rip the posters down, and I would go back to the same spots and replace them. It was like cleaning windows and having someone follow you around and spit on them once you're finished. It was totally fruitless. I figured I wouldn't have a job though if no one went around ripping them down.

That day at work, I went around taping signs on everything. I taped one to a statue of a man riding a horse. It said TESOL in big letters on the sign. I taped some onto trees in the park. I taped about twenty in the bathroom where I went to get a few afternoon pints. I usually walked around for about three and a half hours and charged five. I worked a little less this day. When I got home, Lily's clothes were gone. That was mostly all she had at our place. She must have left work early so that we wouldn't run into each other again.

The following day, I thought about quitting my job and going back to school. I have a tendency to do this when I'm feeling particularly cornered and depressed. As I was taping up posters, mostly on lampposts this time, I found a poster advertising an upcoming stand-up comedy/burlesque show. Lily was slated to perform in it. We had barely spoken for weeks, so I forgot about it till I saw her name on the sign. Lily wasn't particularly funny. At least I didn't think so. I'm not just saying she wasn't funny because I feel indisposed to say anything complimentary about her. She has many fine qualities. True enough, I do not feel inclined to praise her finer points, such as her contagious levity or her statuesque figure or her passionate kindness and compassion, but suffice it to say that funny was not on top of the list. Nevertheless, she moonlighted as an actress and performer. Small-time, mostly unpaid gigs. She got a kick out of it, and I suppose she wasn't terrible.

I ripped down the poster, not in some pitiful gesture but because I intended to go. One of the things Lily used to complain about was how I didn't support her and her acting. I didn't think it realistic that I would win Lily back or anything, but it seemed harmless to attend her show. I got home and mounted it on the fridge with a magnet. It was not for a couple days yet, so I'd have to trudge through the muck for a while longer before seeing her.

My lonesome life was so uneventful that there was very little to report about the intervening days. I pasted more posters during the day, and I spent the nights sitting on the couch, getting drunk and hatching grandiose plans that died as quickly as they materialized. The one plan that lasted longest, for perhaps the better part of an evening, was that I'd move to a Scandinavian country and become a taxi driver. I cannot presently say why Scandinavia, but I suppose I had an idea that Scandinavia was as close to purgatory as any place on Earth. I imagined myself in some city such as Oslo, driving around a road that circumscribed a canal, around and around in circles, picking up and dropping off a cast of nondescript characters until the grooves from my continual course became forged in the cement and I no longer had to even steer the car.

It was a Thursday night, the night of Lily's performance. The event was held at a bar with a stage and very high ceilings. I was a bit early and sat at the bar and ordered a beer. The place got to about three-quarters full by the time the show was set to start. The bar was at the opposite end from the stage. I spun my chair around and watched as the performance began.

The first performer was some sort of hula-hoopist. She had one hula hoop going that she transferred to different parts of her body while she removed pieces of her clothing. As she'd hula-hoop with her knees, she'd remove her shirt. She'd hula-hoop with her neck and remove her pants. I failed to comprehend the point of the performance.

The next few acts were equally bizarre. One guy balanced a chair on his chin as he removed his pants. He ended up in a jockstrap with his naked rear end facing the crowd. Another performance featured a silent couple sitting at a table, eating raw meat as they sat there naked. There were other performances that were equally remarkable and confounding, but they elude me at the moment. I had drunk at least five beers by the time Lily came on stage.

Lily came out wearing a wedding dress. She stood in front of a blank white screen. There was a projector set up in front of the stage that started to whirr as they shut off all the lights. Behind and *on* Lily, the video began to play. It began with a horse running through an open field. The camera zoomed out to reveal an outdoor canopy and a wedding procession. It zoomed in on the bride and groom, and in the video was Lily marrying some guy I'd never seen before. In the video, Lily was smiling and laughing, and close-ups showed Lily lovingly touching the husband. On stage, Lily wore a dead stare, one I had seen before, and she began to apply scarlet lipstick on her lips. The video continued to play the scene from the wedding, as the couple was standing at the altar, and Lily was applying this lipstick on stage and drawing big red lips on her face, like clown's makeup.

Lily started walking towards the front of the stage, pretending to be greeting people at a wedding. "Hi. How are you?" she said. "So glad you could make it." "Oh, thank you. You look wonderful too." She looked a bit creepy with her big red clown lips, paying compliments to the empty space in front of her. Then she took up a position in the middle of the stage. She was standing there, looking extremely serious again, as the projected wedding continued to play on and behind her. She took the straps of the dress off of her shoulders slowly, looking morose. She bent down to grab the bottom of her wedding dress and then pulled the entire dress over her head. She then stood on the stage with her sloppy red lips, wearing only panties, a bra, and white high-heeled shoes. She let her hair down. The priest, meanwhile, was silently reading vows in the projected image. Lily, with the wedding dress already strewn at her feet, took her shoes, her bra, and then, a little startlingly, her panties off, and she stood there naked, looking sad, morose, ridiculous, while the image of her false beautiful wedding played on her body. Lily had a beautiful figure; she was Venus with limbs. She stood as still as a statue. She didn't cover up, simply stood there until the projector's whirr and light died. When they flicked the house lights again, Lily was gone. The show ended like that.

I made the long walk home, but I didn't mind. The night felt full of possibility. I crossed paths with many beautiful women. I imagined their beautiful naked bodies next to mine. I imagined them imagining me with them. They loved me. They wanted to take me home and kiss me. They were not just lookers. They were multi-faceted. They had many excellent facets. I wanted to know them all. "I want to know all your facets," I'd say. "Show me. Show me everything. Show me now."

THE BARISTA AND I

I was standing outside and I was smiling because it was sunny. It was delightful just to stand and smile and look at the firmament which was surely a firmament. I had no doubts that the sky opened into something altogether more spectacular and the space beyond that was a firmament too that opened into something altogether more spectacular than what lay immediately beyond the skies. I knew this because I felt it and I have never felt anything that was not right and true.

I went to a café smiling and the people inside the café were laughing and smiling and I gleamed in their direction and they shone their pearly whites back at me. The barista making my latté was smiling too and she was lovely and I smiled at her and told her that we should go smiling together sometime. We could smile on a sunny day outside together and witness the sky smiling and everything would be delightful and we would stand at the altar together under a shining moon smiling and I would put a scintillating ring on her finger and she would put a scintillating ring on mine.

The barista said she would love to continue smiling and that she would smile with me and that we would smile together forever and ever until we entered the firmament that lay beyond the visible sky. I held her hand lightly and lifted gently and she floated over the counter separating us into my arms and I held her like a baby and the patrons smiled at us as I carried my barista in my arms out of the café into the day.

The barista and I walked along grass roads and admired the fields of sunflowers reaching towards the sun because the sun is god. I told the barista that I thought it was unfair that the sunflowers, though they reach, stay rooted to the ground so that they cannot reach god, that no matter how straight they stretch, their roots remain in the soil. So the barista and I walked into the field and set the sunflowers free. We pulled their roots from the ground one by one and witnessed them floating up to the sun which was god and the sunflowers were even more erect as they floated straight towards the sun (which was god).

The barista and I walked down the grassy roads to a beach for a picnic. The fish were jumping out of the water with big smiles on their faces. The seagulls sang a symphonic tune. Another bird sang from a tree "Pretty girl, pretty girl, pretty girl." The bird sang to the barista of course and she sang back at the bird "Pretty bird, pretty bird, pretty bird." I laughed and the barista laughed and the bird laughed and the fish jumped out of the water laughing. I waded out into the water with the barista and dipped my hands shaped like a cup into the water. And my hands were a cup, a wineglass more precisely, and the water was wine more precisely, and the seagulls were vegetable kebabs more precisely roasting on an open fire that I made on the beach. And the sun was actually the moon and I was actually in love and the barista said "I love you too actually" and everything was very actual and I felt good and I knew that it was good and right and true because I felt it.

We ate the kebabs that were not seagulls and fed some to the fish which were actually golden retrievers and drank the wine which was not water, and the fish that were fish and the birds that were birds smiled. I told the barista that I had a house that was really and truly a house and that it was just across the water and the barista suggested we take the canoe that I had been portaging all day as we picked sunflowers and drank wine and smiled. I laughed because the barista was such a romantic wanting to take a canoe when I had already done all the preparation for us to sail a yacht across. My barista was so imaginative and capricious and I told her and she kissed me because she is impulsive and romantic and wanted to take the canoe and I said "Of course, my sweet, sweet barista."

And so we walked across the water which was water and it soaked my feet but my trousers were rolled up and the barista was barefoot because she always wore a dress the colour of a sun. As we walked I picked her petunias that were growing on the surface of the water and I asked her if she liked petunias and she said she loved them and I told her "I love you, barista, and if you take these petunias you have no obligation to marry me but would you marry me if I gave them to you?" And it was not a trick and it was not a tactic and it was only actual and true and the barista said "I will only accept these petunias if you will marry me tonight and put a brilliantly shining ring on my finger" and I was kneeling down, getting my knee wet in the water and it was all because I was proposing and when you are proposing it looks particularly good in a cir-cumstance like when your knee is getting wet because it shows just how much a thing like wet knees matters compared to an eternal bond and shining rings and smiling skies.

I accepted to marry her and she accepted to marry me and we were at my house and I had set up an altar already and there was not a priest but the moon and the sun would unite us and we would sign our signatures in the water and it would be binding and true and beautiful. I stood before her and gave her a speech that was not so much extemporaneous because it was written in my heart already and I said:

"Sweetest sweet barista, I have known from the very first, even before we picked sunflowers and before we drank wine that was not water and before we ate vegetable kebabs that were not seagulls and before the birds sang to you on the beach that you were the most divine person in your dress the colour of the sun and that I was born to be here giving this speech that is not so much extemporaneous because it is written in my heart and take me to put a shining ring on your finger because we will smile and I will love you and I will walk across grass fields and water and drink wine just to be with you and I will sing to you and be my wife, sweet barista?"

And the barista said "I do."

I kissed the barista and she kissed me and it was chastening and it was perfect and we were united and we signed our names on the contract that was actually water and heard the priest which was actually the sun and the moon legitimize our union and I made love sweet love to the barista on our wedding bed which was actually a sunny field and the sky smiled and the animals smiled and the barista smiled and I smiled and we both orgasmed simultaneously and then there was nothing and we ascended towards the firmament only to go beyond that to the beyond which is also a firmament to live in the beyond beyond and we have scintillating rings and I know everything will be perfect because I felt it and I thought it and my barista knows it and feels it too.

Some Kind of
Second Coming

Every phone and alarm and radio and TV and doorbell and car engine and megaphone and every noise-emitting device everywhere in the known world and the unknown world went off all at once. A man in Tuvalu was struck in the head by a falling coconut. A man in Honduras heard the sound of a million guns being discharged at once. A woman in France heard the screams of a thousand orgasms. Every animal in the world, domestic and still undomesticated, tired and high-strung, endangered and overpopulated, let out the sound each makes. An elephant in the Central African Republic blew water from his trunk and made his elephant noise, as did all the other elephants in the C.A.R. and everywhere else in the world. So did all the dogs in the world bark, all the cats meow, all the bullfrogs make that throaty noise, all the flies buzz. So did all of everything do everything. The millions of people on Facebook were all poked simultaneously by an unknown contact. Every person's status was liked. Google had a mysterious new doodle of rosary beads. Beds shook, the wind blew, trees canted, a man in America could hear distantly U2's "Vertigo." Everyone in the world, despite the time of day, for the first time in all the history of the world, every single living person was awake. Every electronic device awakened. Stereos not even plugged in, without batteries, came to life. Imagine your face in front of a TV without reception, and a radio between stations—now imagine your head inside the TV, inside the static, and your head inside the radio between stations, your mind a big staticky void, your eyes a blank white screen. Imagine everyone in the world feeling the exact same thing. Even a child in the unmapped jungle of Brazil who has never seen or heard of a TV or a radio is experiencing the exact same thing as you. People's thoughts, always obstructed and simplified by imperfect means of communication, emanated from them like a gazillion invisible tendrils. There was no longer this inherent failure, that attempt to squeeze a thousand watermelons through a single keyhole all at once. Everywhere in the world, people's billions upon billions of simultaneous thoughts reaching everyone else. People, animals, trees, every living thing, and every inanimate thing, for inanimate things are made up of atoms too—every living and every non-living thing revealed itself to be pure energy. As people shucked off their bodies like corn husks, the bodies all convened in the centre of the world, making unabashed love to each other, unprejudiced undiscerning love, with no anxieties, uninhabited even by the people, who had turned into pure energy, who were those tendrils that were thoughts and emotions and conflicting thoughts and conflicting emotions, and everyone who came close enough to experience this other person, who came within his or her orbit, understood everything of the other at once. All at once and instantaneously and everywhere on Earth, everyone understood everything about everyone else. The people, pure sources of energy and light, emanated messages of understanding—I understand you, it's okay, everything is okay, in fact everything is better than okay now that I know everything about you, I can forgive you, can forgive anything. And the millions upon millions of atoms making up each of the millions upon millions of sources of energy and light all gathered in the centre of the universe, which is to say the centre of nowhere, and it could not be said that one thing was not another thing, that another thing was outside of this thing, could not be said that there were things at all—that in fact the message of so many things like religion and philosophy was true, that everything is not just everything but everything else too.

PEOPLE I HARDLY KNOW

I woke up late, at almost 2 p.m. I wanted to go to the laundromat/café to speak to the girl who worked there. Her shift ended at 4 p.m, so I felt I had to rush. I had been going to the laundromat for a while now because I was en-amoured of the girl.

Leila was French. I loaned her a book by an American writer a few weeks ago because she wanted to improve her English, and she had noticed me often reading there. Leila came over to me the week before when I was reading *Gravity's Rainbow* and asked me what it was about, how I was liking it, and if she could borrow it after I was finished. I told her she could but that it could prove very difficult for her to read, as her English was as poor as my French, though I didn't tell her that. What I did say was that I didn't understand it and English is my first language. The reason she wanted to read the book was because she liked this band, much like an orchestra, composed of approximately thirty musicians playing a wide variety of instruments, who named their latest album after Pynchon's latest book, *Against the Day*.

I walked into the laundromat with a garbage bag full of dirty whites slung over my shoulder. She greeted me warmly. I asked her how she was doing and ordered two portions of laundry soap and an allongé.

We barely knew each other, but I felt our relationship was very complex, and depending on the week, she either seemed pleased to see me or flustered and put-off, never neutral. I think she often forgot how hopeless my French was, as she spoke quickly and nervously and smilingly. I didn't know when she was finished what she was saying, as I only ever caught a few of the words.

I might not have thought about Leila much if I had many friends or conversations, but I didn't, so I did. She was delicate and smiley and kind of debonair-seeming. She seemed a bit in her own head, but it must have been a pleasant place, for outwardly she came off so free of self-consciousness and sadness. She had wide-open eyes that were friendly but a bit distant.

I was standing at the counter, and she brought me my allongé. She had topped it with milk and sprinkled chocolate on it.

"I'm sorry," I said in my poor French, "but I can't eat chocolate."

She said some words much too quickly in French and dumped it in the sink, and she began to make me another. I walked over to the laundry machines and filled two of them with my clothes, paid the machines, and returned to the counter.

Leila gave me my new allongé, apologizing and looking dejected.

I sat at the counter, and very few customers came in, so I put my book down and talked with Leila. I wasn't thinking about having sex with her, but I did imagine that it would be nice to find her dark hair on my pillow when I woke. She was slender and lithe. Whenever she bent down to get something behind the counter, she would bend from the waist, hardly at all at the knees.

From our conversation, what I understood was that she was in her second year of university, but her professors were on strike. She studied sociology, though she said she was not particularly interested in anything academic. Our conversation became confused and stilted after a short while, so she busied herself behind the counter and I attended to my laundry and read.

Leila was replaced at 4 p.m. by an unfriendly girl. Leila gathered her coat and backpack when the new girl arrived and walked around the counter. She stopped as she passed me and began to speak. She looked very shy all of a sudden, and she told me that the band with the album *Against the Day* was playing on Tuesday.

"Are you inviting me?" I asked.

"If you want," she said.

"I'll be there."

I asked for her phone number, saying that I would call her Tuesday evening to meet beforehand for a drink. She wrote it on a napkin for me and left.

I didn't stay very much longer, because my laundry was finished. I thought about Leila that night and about all the women I had ever gone out with, which wasn't all that many. I fell asleep late, which was okay because I didn't work in the morning. I worked from home, editing technical documents for a company where I had worked on-site for a year doing a nine-to-five. Work had been slow, but I didn't need much money to live.

When I awoke on Monday, I had to pack a bag and walk to an apartment where I had agreed to look after a cat for a few days. I arrived at the apartment, and the concierge let me in. He was expecting me. His name was Pablo, and he unlocked the door to the apartment for me. The cat was waiting by the door, meowing, and the keys had been left for me on the kitchen table.

It felt strange being in this acquaintance's apartment. I had only met her twice and been in the apartment once. She had got my number from a mutual acquaintance. She must have been desperate for someone to look after her cat. I leafed through her record collection and her books and fed the cat. I felt like a burglar or a voyeur. I ordered in food and listened to records and drank a pot of coffee over the course of the evening.

Tuesday came, still without work. I stayed in bed until late and then went grocery shopping after feeding the cat. I made myself some spaghetti and had a cigarette out on the balcony. I bided my time, listening to records I had never heard of, until it was an appropriate time to call Leila.

I sat on the couch with the music on, and the cat sat there next to me, looking bored or tired. I retrieved the napkin that Leila had written on, and I called the number. An automated voice came on that informed me that the number was not currently in use. I tried again, thinking I had misdialled, but got the same automated voice. I immediately thought that she must have given me a fake phone number, but then it seemed bizarre that she would go out of her way to invite me to a concert and not give me a real number. I was dumbfounded and a bit deflated. It didn't make any sense.

I went to the fridge, and the cat followed me. I got a beer and went back to the couch, where the cat returned to his former position, next to me, swinging his tail so it'd hit my bare forearms. I put on a new record and continued drinking on the couch until it was time to leave for the concert.

I left my house at the time the concert was set to begin. I didn't want to arrive before Leila. When I got to the venue, the band had not yet started. There were a few chairs arranged in a semi-circle. I ordered a beer and walked the circumference of the chairs. They were all occupied even though the band hadn't started. Leila wasn't there yet, so I went out for a cigarette, hoping to catch her on her way in. I peered in both directions as I smoked because I didn't know which direction she would be coming from.

It was 8:45 by the time I got back inside, and the band still hadn't begun to play. I ordered another beer and stood at the bar, surveying the place. I was beginning to feel a bit drunk, and I just wanted the music to start. It wasn't until I was almost finished my third beer that the band started to play. People kept showing up intermittently, usually in clumps, through the first few long songs. I felt lousy, but at least the music had begun.

I finally saw Leila come in, but I felt so confused and lousy that it took me a while to go over to her. It appeared that she came alone, which was good, but I still didn't feel great about the whole situation. We greeted each other, a bit coldly, while the band finished one of their songs. The band was decent, original, but frankly I just wanted it to end so that I could maybe get some things cleared up.

After the band finished, I asked Leila if she wanted a drink. She said no thanks, so I went to the bar and ordered myself another beer. While I was waiting for my beer, she came up to the bar and asked for water. We sat down in some of the recently vacated chairs in the semi-circle. Leila's eyes were darting all around, and she seemed to be drifting in and out of attention in our conversation, so it was even more disjointed than usual. She said something I didn't comprehend about needing to ask someone in the crowd a question, and she got up abruptly and left.

She came back a few minutes later. I told her I had tried to call her earlier but that the number she gave me didn't exist. She said, as though it were an answer, that she moved around a lot. I wanted to ask what exactly that meant, but she didn't seem in the mood to really discuss it. Leila betrayed some interest, became animated, when we spoke about the performance we'd just seen. She told me that she made music on strange instruments that her grandfather had invented. Our conversation dissolved after that, and Leila recognized a friend standing at the bar and went over to talk to her.

Nothing had been explained, and I still felt confused. I got up from my seat and approached her at the bar. I told her that I was going to go see an old friend deejay at a bar nearby.

"What type of music?" she asked.

It was '50s soul music.

She said she wasn't feeling up to it. I left her with her friend and began walking alone. I didn't end up going to see my friend deejay.

I went home and went to bed instead.

I got some work on Wednesday. The company that I edited documents for was attending an international conference, and they were releasing a bunch of products in the new quarter, so I was busy for the rest of the week with the editing.

The woman came back to her apartment on Saturday. She thanked me for watching the cat, making the observation that he (the cat) seemed better adjusted than when she had left. I found it hard to believe, but I accepted her compliment and returned home.

I stayed in Saturday night, drinking wine, as I had nothing to do, and returned to the laundromat the next day. I didn't go to figure anything out, and certainly not to make Leila uncomfortable, but just to show that there was no harm done.

Leila acted a bit nervous when I ordered an allongé from her. She didn't mention the concert or the book I had loaned her. I went to a distant table in the café and sat down to read.

Leila called me over to the counter after

about a half an hour, and she said, "This is my little sister." I looked and saw nothing, no one. I was confused. I suspected she really was off in some way. But as I walked closer, I saw a little girl who didn't reach the counter, standing between her sister's legs.

"Oh," I said. "Hi."

The little girl was shy and didn't say anything. Leila smiled at me, and then I went back to my table, and I heard her asking her little sister if she wanted anything to eat.

I went out for a smoke and came back to my table. When I got back in, Leila came over and asked me if I'd mind if her friend sat with me at the table (across from me was an empty seat).

"Sure," I said.

A girl came over with pages of study notes and sat down.

"Thanks," she said. "It is pretty hard to concentrate sitting at the counter."

Her English was good, much better than Leila's.

She laid out her papers and asked me if I was working too.

"No," I said. "Just reading."

"Would it be intrusive if I asked you what you were reading?"

I showed her the cover of *The Savage Detectives* by Bolaño.

"I have never heard of him," she said.

I asked her what she was studying.

"Osteopathy," she said. "It is used to treat people with pain. In the body. A lot of people confuse it with homeopathy, but it is not the same thing. Osteopathy treats pain by looking at the mind and the body."

"Hmm," I said. "How long is the program?"

"It is six years," she said. "I am only in my second year. There are some programs that are only two years, but I would not feel comfortable treating people after only two years. This one is long, but it all depends on how you look at it. It is not so bad. I just try not to think about the next four years. I just try to concentrate on what I am doing now, and it is not so bad."

"It's always that way, isn't it?" I said. "It's not so bad if you can find a good way to think about it. You can really take the pressure off that way."

She asked me if I had a cigarette, and so I went with her outside in the courtyard to have a smoke. The courtyard had wooden benches all around the interior of a wooden fence, and we sat in a corner.

"It's a nice neighbourhood here," I said.

"Yes," she said. "You live here?"

"Yes," I said. "You too?"

"Yes. I was living way east before. My old neighbourhood was poor, and people walked around slouched. I have, like, a melancholic disposition, I think. So I would see the people walking around, and the streets were never cleaned, and everybody started to just make me really depressed, and I had to move. I thought that the people in this neighbourhood would be snotty and phony and arrogant, but I find it has not been that way at all."

"No. It's really quite nice," I said.

We sat and finished our cigarettes and put them out in an old tin can next to the bench we were sitting on. We just sat a few minutes before going inside. When we did go inside, she started working again, and I kept reading. Four o'clock came, and Leila was leaving from her shift. She said goodbye to her friend and me and then left. She came back a few minutes later to get her hat, which she had forgotten, and when she was leaving again, she stopped, and she apologized. I thought she was apologizing to her friend for something, but then I looked up from my book and she was talking to me.

"Sorry," she said. "Sorry about before. I wasn't myself. I feel pretty bad about it. I wasn't feeling right."

She said goodbye and left.

I stayed at the café despite Leila's departure. The presence of her friend was comfortable. I didn't have anything to do for the rest of the day. After a while spent in silence, reading, I had finished my coffee. My laundry was dry in the machine, and I went to pack it into a garbage bag that I used to carry my laundry to and from the laundromat. I came back to the table and sat down a minute. I felt connected to this girl whose name I didn't even know. I would have liked to see her again. She was busy studying, and I was tired of reading, so I decided I'd leave. I thought it unlikely that I'd ever see this girl again, as I didn't want to ask for her phone number and I didn't want to go out on a date with her. What we had was enough.

I got up to leave and asked her for her name.

"Maude," she said.

"It was nice to meet you, Maude."

I held out my hand, and she took it and then placed her other hand on top of the back of my hand. When she released my hand, I turned towards the door and waved back at her. When I got outside, I felt warm, and I didn't really feel bad at all.

ON WANTING TO LOOK LIKE
YOU HAVE IT ALL TOGETHER

The thing is, you keep telling yourself, the thing is, is that it's not so bad, really, when you think about it, when you think about so many other things that are much worse, like wretched squalor and public humiliation. No, things aren't so bad, you think, hauling on a cigarette, sitting in the bleachers. But you shouldn't be smoking. No, your lungs are going rotten already, already in your twenties, your lungs are rotting and becoming thick like molasses. But, you reason, but yes, I started later, you say to yourself, later than most of the other smokers I know, and so I get to smoke guilt-free for a few more years, until I find a reason to quit. Like you'll quit if you get your girlfriend pregnant, you think. And you think, but I don't have a girlfriend. But, you think, sitting on the bleachers near the outdoor hockey rink, but there's no reason why I shouldn't have a girlfriend, I'm kind of starting to be a contributing member of society. Sort of, at least. You think, I'm no longer spending whole days in bed and whole nights drunk. No, I'm becoming more reasonable, you think, more disciplined, and now there's probably not as many reasons for me to not have a girlfriend or not be able to have a girlfriend. But I don't know exactly, you find yourself saying, though you don't know why you *say* it, but I don't quite know lately.... With all the changes you've been undergoing, you don't quite now know how to identify yourself, such as just now you've contemplated, though perhaps unseriously, quitting smoking, and now, you think, I'm going to have to find a place to accommodate into my sense of identity these incipient thoughts of quitting smoking. But that's not so much it. That's not really it, you think. No, it's not exactly like that. It's more that I have to accommodate into my identity this new knowledge that I'm the type of person who contemplates quitting smoking. One thing at a time, you think. Yes, first you can accommodate the fact that you're the type of person who would consider quitting smoking, and then should you ever commit to that idea that you had, that you should quit smoking, then you could further incorporate this smoking disinclination into your person. But one thing at a time.

Watching the snow-covered skating rink, lighting another cigarette, sitting in the bleachers, you think, how did I come to be the person on this side of the boards? Have I become a spectator, you think, now that I'm not on the other side of the boards, that I'm not shovelling the rink and playing hockey? Am I a spectator in life now that I don't shovel the rink and play hockey, when before I was always shovelling rinks and always playing hockey? Is this worse, you wonder, sitting here instead of smoking joints and then shovelling and playing hockey? But, no, you think, just because I'm getting myself together doesn't mean I'm a spectator, doesn't mean I'm not an actor, not a player. I'm already thinking about accommodating into my identity thoughts about quitting smoking and even, one day down the line, you think, smoking, acting on those ideas. I've already changed a lot. And all this, you think, I've thought while sitting alone in the bleachers.

And though I've come a long way, you think, already in a few minutes, have changed really quite a lot, am I ready to absorb and incorporate these changes? you wonder, exhaling smoke. Am I ready to be this type of person who can conceive of a life without smoking? But, I already am, you think, because I've already conceived it. And you sit there, wondering just who you are, just how different you are from earlier that day at work, when you were wondering if you were really the type of person who could hold down a job, who might be able to interact with others and participate as a cog in a machine and really work. To your astonishment, though, it was apparent that you had been working, had been working there quite some time already, and that made you think about how you were being dehumanized for a pittance, and it made you envy every drunk at all the bars when you walked home along the main street. And you were just starting to incorporate into yourself the idea that you were somebody who walks now, but I used to sit there, you thought, walking past the bars, I used to sit there, and there, and there, often and sometimes for long periods of time. Who was that who would just sit there drinking? Did he think about getting a job? you wonder. And you recall that that's how you got where you are now, walking and working. You got to walking and working because you started thinking about those things when you were sitting and drinking. But how did you get to sitting and drinking so often, sometimes for long periods of time? Before that, what was there? You had a girlfriend some time ago. It took you a long time to incorporate the reality that you were a person without a girlfriend, that you were someone who was disgusting to many women, sitting and drinking and behaving badly. Did she have anything to do with it? you think now. She almost certainly did, you think. You think, lighting a cigarette, that where you got to now almost certainly has something to do with her. It has something to do, you think, with her, but mostly with her being gone. Yes, all this, sitting here on these bleachers, you think, almost certainly has to do with her. This walking and working, she has everything to do with it. But she is not here, you think. She hasn't been around for a long time. You wonder how long it's been. You think, this is all because of her. The next time you see her, you think, smoking a cigarette after work on the bleachers in an empty park, the next time you see her, you will show her just how much you've changed.

Acknowledgments

Thanks to Mikhail Iossel for supervising my thesis and helping shape these stories; to Jon Paul Fiorentino for finding this book a home and editing it; and to Josip Novakovich for encouragement and feedback. Thanks to my elder John Goldbach for some advice. And big thanks to the Insomniac folks.

Immeasurable thanks to my parents, Leon and Suzana, and my brother Nate, for everything (including, in Nate's case, some keen editorial insights). And Katie Chiarelli, for a good run. And hugely to Alex Laidlaw, without whom I doubt I'd be writing.

The story "Body Language" was influenced by David Foster Wallace's story collection *Brief Interviews with Hideous Men.*

"The Barista and I" originally appeared in *Matrix* and later in translation in *Timarit Máls og menningar* (thanks to Atli Bollason for translating it).

www.ingramcontent.com/pod-product-compliance
Lightning Source LLC
Chambersburg PA
CBHW061635050726

47502CB00012B/2236